This book belongs to

_____

For Tyler and his duck

Text © 1991 by Angela Elwell Hunt
Illustrations © 1991 by Natalie Carabetta
Library of Congress catalog number 91-65155
ISBN 0-8423-0302-2
Printed in Mexico
98 97 96 95 94 93 92 91
9 8 7 6 5 4 3 2 1

Calico Bear

By *Angela Elwell Hunt*

Illustrated by Natalie Carabetta

TYNDALE HOUSE PUBLISHERS, INC.
WHEATON, ILLINOIS

 e wasn't sure how it happened, but suddenly Calico Bear felt happy and loved. He was in the arms of a smiling boy who squeezed him tightly and squealed, "Thank you, Daddy! He's a beautiful bear!"

From that moment on, Calico Bear spent all his time with Tyler. They shared many adventures during the day. But Calico Bear's favorite time was when they snuggled down to sleep at night. After Tyler said his prayers, he placed Calico Bear in the crook of his left arm. Then his mother tucked them in and sang a quiet song:

Sleep, my child, and never fear:
God's constant love will keep you near.
And as you grow a bit each day,
God's loving hands will guide your way.

After a time, Calico Bear and Tyler began to change. Tyler grew inches taller. He ran faster and played harder. Calico Bear was not able to keep up.

Calico Bear's button eyes loosened and popped off. His calico skin faded after many tumbles in the washing machine. He was afraid Tyler would forget all about him. But Tyler still loved Calico Bear.

One day Tyler's friend Joey came to play. "What an ugly old bear!" said Joey, pointing to Calico Bear. "Why do you keep it? You don't play with that baby toy, do you?"

Tyler did not answer.

That night Tyler's mother began to tuck Calico Bear and Tyler into bed. "Mom," Tyler said, "I don't think I need to sleep with Calico Bear anymore. And you don't have to tuck me in anymore, either."

Tyler's mother smiled. "I see. You're a big boy now, aren't you?"

Tyler nodded.

Mother sat on the bed and gently held Calico Bear. "What shall I do with your bear?" she asked.

"I don't need any baby toys," Tyler whispered. "But please don't throw him out."

Mother thought a moment. "Calico Bear looks too tired to be a toy," she said. "Maybe it's time for him to have a new job."

She kissed Tyler good night and turned out the light.

Tyler's mother knew just what to do with a tired toy bear. She carefully cut Calico Bear's seams and removed the old, matted stuffing. She cut Calico Bear's fabric into tiny squares and stitched them together with other fabric squares. As she stitched, she sang the familiar lullaby:

> *Sleep, my child, and never fear:*
> *God's constant love will keep you near.*
> *And as you grow a bit each day,*
> *God's loving hands will guide your way.*

When the quilt was done, she placed it on Tyler's bed.

"A Calico Bear quilt!" exclaimed Tyler when he saw it. "Thanks, Mom."

That night Tyler tucked himself in and slept, safe and warm, with Calico Bear in the quilt over the crook of his left arm.

Tyler slept under Calico Bear's quilt every night for many years. When Tyler grew up and moved away, the quilt was carefully folded and placed in a box in the attic. For a long time, Calico Bear wondered if he would ever see Tyler again.

Then one day someone lifted Calico Bear's quilt out of the box. "What a lovely quilt!" a young and pretty lady said to Tyler's mother. "But it is worn out. May I use it?"

Tyler's mother touched the quilt and hummed the old lullaby. "You're part of our family now," she said. "You may have the quilt."

Calico Bear could hardly wait to see Tyler, but instead he was taken downstairs to the sewing room. The young lady began to cut the quilt. She cut out triangles, ovals, circles, and rectangles. *Whirrrr* went the sewing machine as she sewed the pieces together and filled them with new, soft stuffing.

Calico Bear's new button eyes sparkled. He was once again a small bear! His skin was quilted now, and he had a black embroidered nose. His ears were lined with shiny pink satin, and he had a tiny tongue of bright red felt.

He wasn't sure how it happened, but suddenly Calico Bear felt happy and loved. He was in the arms of a smiling girl in pajamas who squeezed him tightly and squealed, "Thank you, Mommy! He's a beautiful bear!"

The small girl, who looked very much like Tyler, squeezed Calico Bear again and carried him up into her big bed. There she slept, safe and warm, with Calico Bear in the crook of her left arm. And Tyler, now grown tall, sang the familiar lullaby to his daughter:

Sleep, my child, and never fear:

God's constant love will keep you near.

And as you grow a bit each day,

God's loving hands will guide your way.